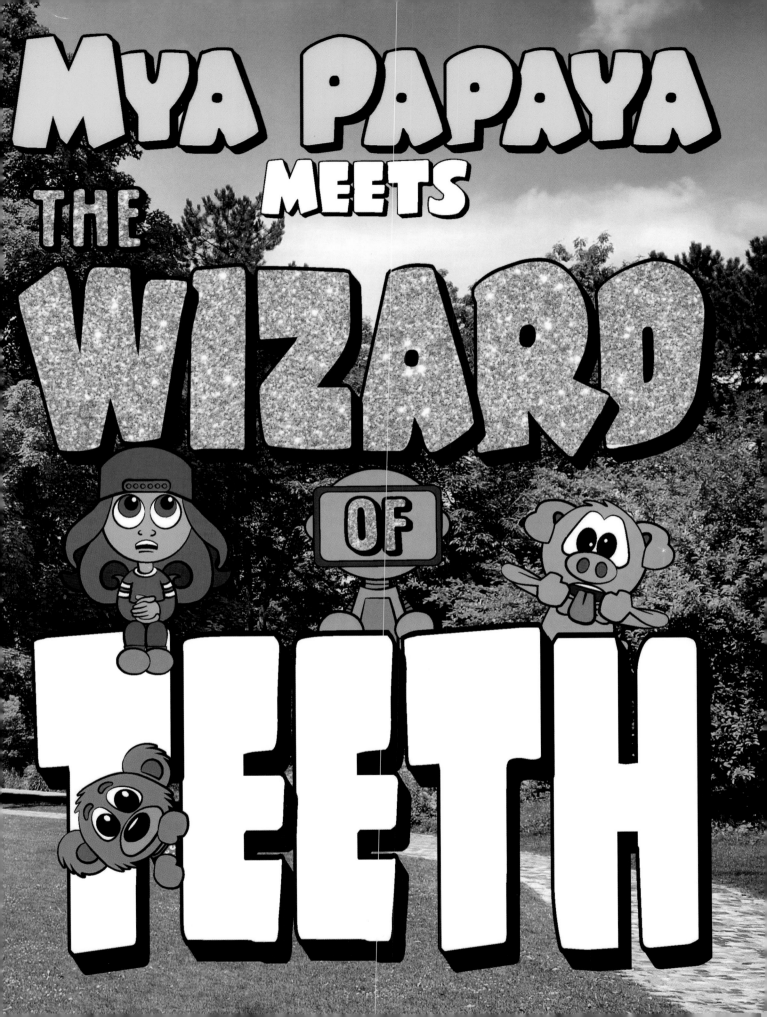

Archway Publishing books may be ordered through booksellers or by contacting:

Archway Publishing
1663 Liberty Drive
Bloomington, IN 47403
www.archwaypublishing.com
1 (888) 242-5904

Art by Jim Wojdyla.

ISBN: 978-1-4808-6529-7 (sc)
ISBN: 978-1-4808-6528-0 (hc)
ISBN: 978-1-4808-6530-3 (e)

Printed in the United States of America.

Archway Publishing rev. date: 8/29/2018

JIM WOJDYLA

Mr. Jim loves reading to his own kids and to elementary school classrooms, as a guest reader, and being fun and interactive with the kids. It helps him keep his playful imagination and makes him feel like a big kid...Literally...He is 6'8" tall!! Jim is the singer of a popular band in the Chicago area called Modern Day Romeos. They have been playing large festivals for over 15 years. His favorite part of the show is bringing kids up on stage to sing, dance and act silly with him.

DR. TIM STIRNEMAN

Dr. Tim is a dentist and has a practice called Compassionate Dentalcare. He loves kids so much that his office has a special room, JUST for kids, with a big TV to watch cartoons and three TV's to play video games on! He wrote a play called "The Wizard of Teeth" based on his favorite movie "The Wizard of Oz." Every year, Dr. Tim and friends travel to elementary schools to perform this play to thousands of kids! They laugh, have fun, and learn about their teeth and how awesome going to the dentist can be! This play sparked the idea for the Mya Papaya book series.

MR. JIM AND DR. TIM

come from different worlds, but their shared passion for local community outreach is one of the things that brought them together and fueled their desire to become children's book authors. Their daughters, and Dr. Tim's granddaughter, give them their inspiration to bring funny, yet thoughtful and meaningful stories and experiences to life. They also founded two national holidays, National Dental Care Month every May and National Smile Day every May 31st.

WE MUST ALL EMPOWER OUR CHILDREN AND TEACH THEM TO TRY AS MANY NEW THINGS AS POSSIBLE. WHEN THEY FIND SOMETHING THAT THEY LOVE, NO MATTER HOW ORDINARY OR EXTRAORDINARY, ENCOURAGE AND EXCITE THEM INTO BEING THE BEST THAT THEY CAN IMAGINE BEING.

Please share a picture of you with this book on social media with #mayapapaya. We would like to hear your feedback or ideas. Visit our website or email us!

WWW.MYAPAPAYABOOKS.COM
JIMANDTIM@MYAPAPAYABOOKS.COM

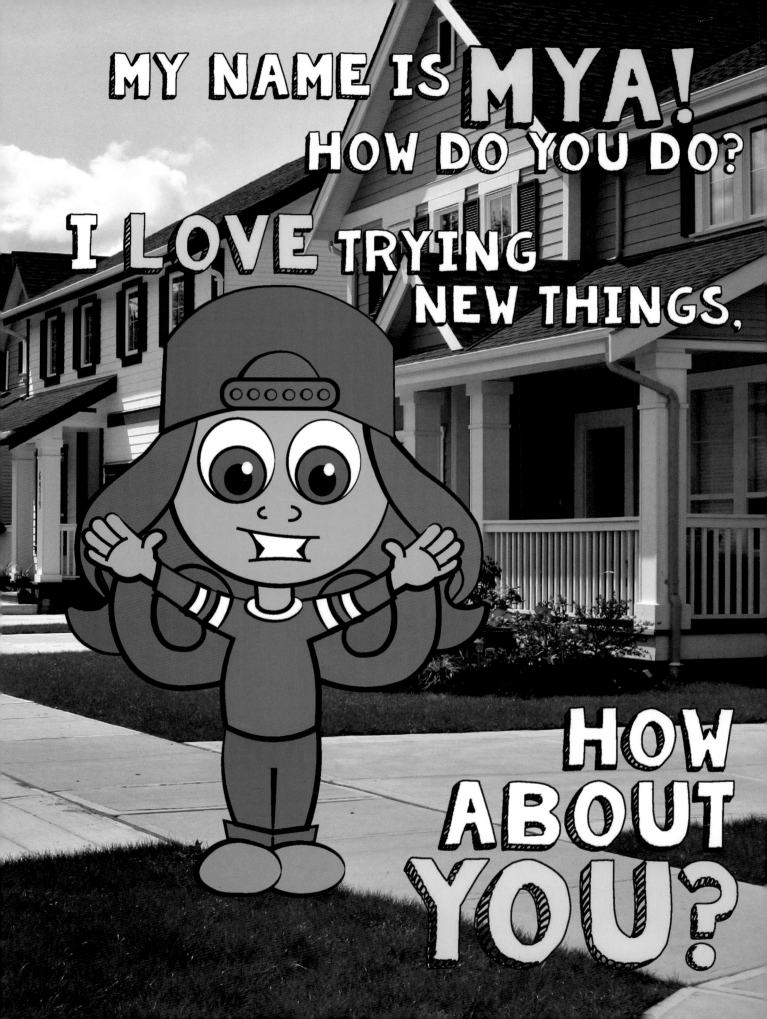

I GO ON MANY ADVENTURES SOME BIG AND SOME SMALL.

MY BEST FRIENDS GO WITH, YOU MUST MEET THEM ALL!

Before turning page two, I'd like you to... say something new, that you've tried too!

HE'S A SCAREDY BEAR WITH ALL KINDS OF THINGS.

HE HIDES WHEN I SNEEZE OR WHEN THE PHONE RINGS.

Can you please share, with Cubbie Bear, a time where, you were very scared?

PAXON IS MY PET.
HE'S AS SILLY AS CAN BE!

ON MY BIRTHDAY,
MY DAD BROUGHT HIM
HOME

JUST
FOR ME!

PAX IS CLUMSY AND PLAYFUL AND ALWAYS HAS FUN!

HE LIVES FOR ADVENTURES AND LOVES EVERY ONE!

I say we take a really quick break. What is the silliest face you can make?

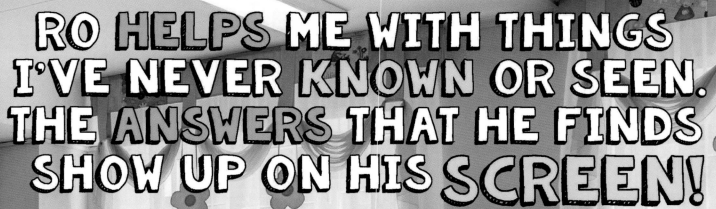

RO HELPS ME WITH THINGS I'VE NEVER KNOWN OR SEEN. THE ANSWERS THAT HE FINDS SHOW UP ON HIS SCREEN!

CHOCOLATE OR VANILLA ICE CREAM... WHICH ONE WAS FIRST CREATED?

IT WAS CHOCOLATE ICE CREAM. THEY MADE IT... THEN THEY ATE IT!

I like to play, and learn everyday! Can you say, what you've learned today?

I DON'T WANT TO BE BORING

SO BEFORE YOU START SNORING

LET'S TURN THE PAGE

AND START THE EXPLORING!

PAX HEARD CRAZY GLASSES POP OUT OF HIS FACE!

HE'S THE WIZARD OF TEETH THAT'S FROM OUTER SPACE!

CUBBIE HEARD THAT THE DENTIST IS A BIG SCARY GUY!

WHEN HE WALKS IN THE ROOM HE'LL MAKE YOUR TEETH CRY!

IT WAS GETTING LATE
SO THEY ALL WENT TO
BED.

BUT
STAYED UP ALL NIGHT
WITH SCARY
THOUGHTS IN THEIR HEAD.

THEY WALKED
IN THE DOOR,
AND AS WIDE
AS A MILE,
WAS A DESK
WITH A LADY

WHO SAID WITH
A SMILE...

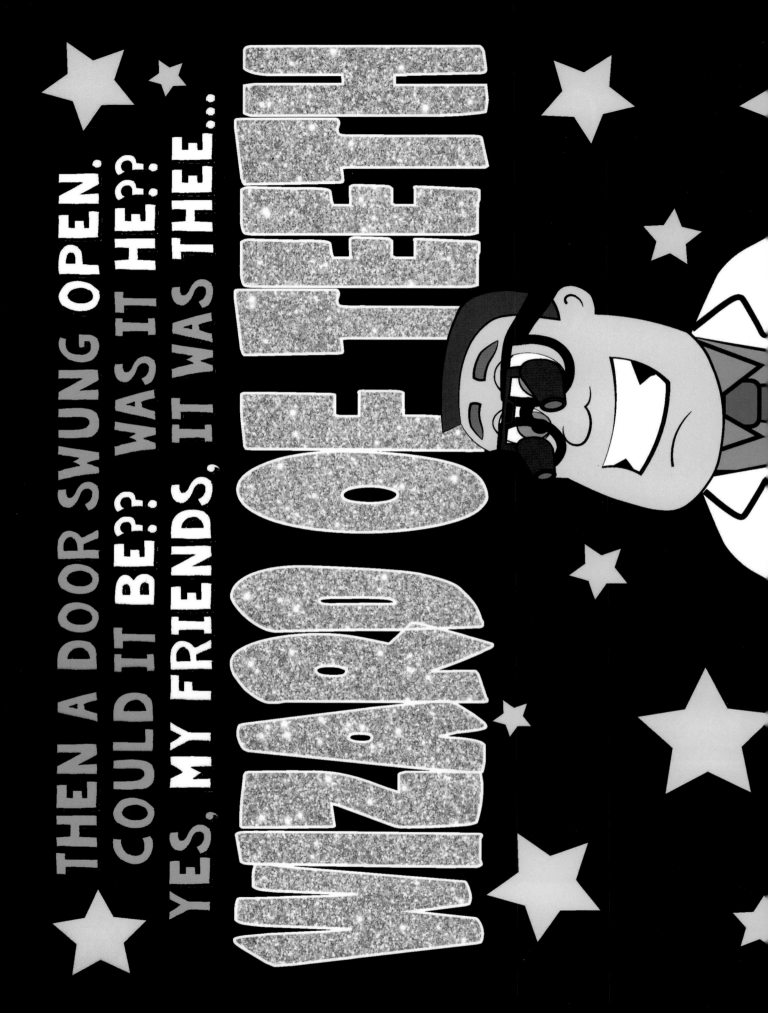

CUBBIE SHOT THE SQUIRT GUN AND PAXON GOT HIT.

MISTER THIRSTY IS A HOSE THAT SUCKS UP YOUR SPIT.

A SPECIAL CAMERA FINDS WHERE ALL YOUR TEETH ARE.

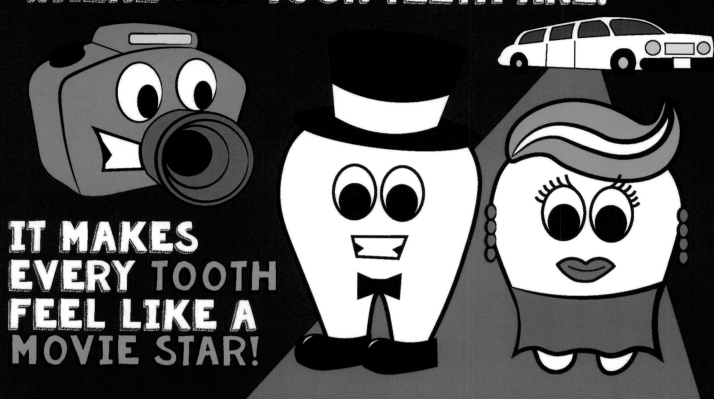

IT MAKES EVERY TOOTH FEEL LIKE A MOVIE STAR!

RIGHT ON RO'S SCREEN WAS AN X-RAY OF MYA'S TEETH,

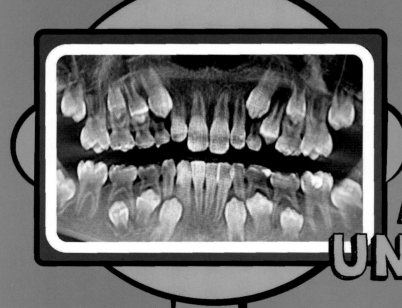

TO SHOW HER WHOLE CLASS THE ADULT TEETH UNDERNEATH.

AND THERE'S SOMEONE ELSE AS **FUN** AS THE DENTIST,

WHO CLEANS UP YOUR TEETH AND IS CALLED A **HYGIENIST!**

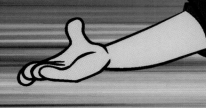

HYGIENIST PRONOUNCED HI-JEN-IST

MYA PAPAYA WAS HAPPY TO HEAR,

THEY WILL NOW VISIT THEIR DENTIST TWICE A YEAR!